You're Speeding Through the Clouds!

It's fun practicing fancy turns and twists high up in the sky. Then you see a spaceship. It is caught in a storm.

Then you look down and discover that there is an earthquake in the town below you.

If you check out the earthquake,
turn to page 12.

If you try to help the spaceship,
turn to page 14.

WHAT WILL HAPPEN NEXT? TURN THE PAGE FOR MORE THRILLS AND FUN!
WHATEVER YOU DO, IT'S UP TO YOU!

WHICH WAY SECRET DOOR Books for you to enjoy

Available from ARCHWAY paperbacks

which way·secret door·books

#1

R.G. Austin

Wow!
You Can Fly!

Illustrated by
Joseph A. Smith

AN ARCHWAY PAPERBACK
Published by POCKET BOOKS · NEW YORK

FOR DOLLY, DAVE,
CAROLYN, DAVID,
AND MELISSA
WITH LOVE

AN ARCHWAY PAPERBACK *Original*

An Archway Paperback published by
POCKET BOOKS, a division of Simon & Schuster, Inc.
1230 Avenue of the Americas, New York, N.Y. 10020

ISBN: 0-671-46979-7

First Archway Paperback printing July, 1983

10 9 8 7 6 5 4 3 2 1

AN ARCHWAY PAPERBACK and colophon are
trademarks of Simon & Schuster, Inc.

WHICH WAY is a registered trademark
of Simon & Schuster, Inc.

SECRET DOOR is a trademark
of Simon & Schuster, Inc.

Printed in the U.S.A.

IL   1+

ATTENTION!

READING A SECRET DOOR BOOK IS LIKE PLAYING A GAME.

HERE ARE THE RULES

Begin reading on page 1. When you come to a choice, decide what to do and follow the directions. Keep reading and following the directions until you come to an ending, then go back to the beginning and make new choices.

There are many stories and many endings in this book.

HAVE FUN!

It is dark outside. You have gone to bed, but you are still wide awake.

You lie quietly until everyone in the house is asleep. Then you creep out of bed and tiptoe into the closet.

You push away the clothes and knock three times on the back wall. Soon the secret door begins to move. It opens just wide enough for you to slip through.

Turn to the next page.

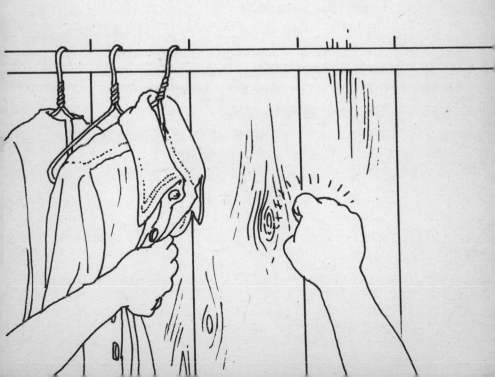

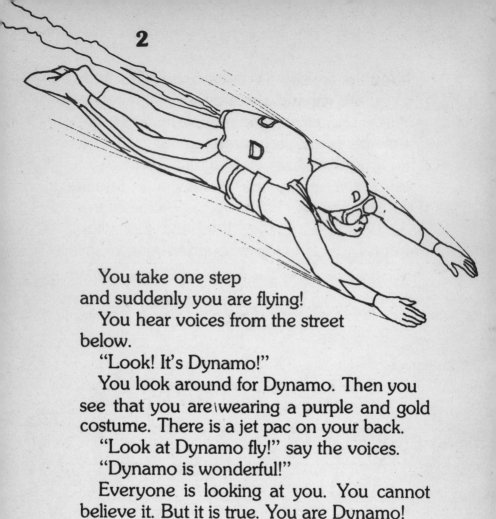

You take one step
and suddenly you are flying!

You hear voices from the street
below.

"Look! It's Dynamo!"

You look around for Dynamo. Then you
see that you are wearing a purple and gold
costume. There is a jet pac on your back.

"Look at Dynamo fly!" say the voices.

"Dynamo is wonderful!"

Everyone is looking at you. You cannot
believe it. But it is true. You are Dynamo!

You fly up. You fly down. You fly in circles.

You are waving at the people below when you see a masked man running out of a bank. He is carrying a money bag.

Uh-oh! A robber, you think.

If you tell the police what is going on, turn to page 4.

If you try to capture the man yourself, turn to page 6.

You jet down to the police station. The police race off in their cars and you fly into the sky.

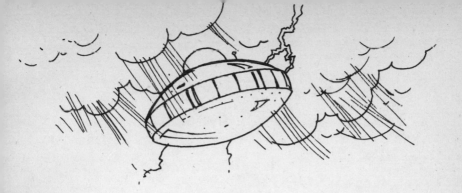

You are practicing fancy turns and twists when you see a spaceship. It is caught in a storm.

You are about to fly to the spacecraft when you look down. Oh, no! There is an earthquake in the town below you.

If you check out the earthquake, turn to page 12.

If you try to help the spaceship, turn to page 14.

6

You fly as fast
as you can toward
the man.

He looks up at you!

"Stay away from me!" he yells. "You are ruining everything!"

If you try to catch the man, turn to page 8.

If you try to kick the money bag out of his hand, turn to page 10.

You fly straight at the robber. You grab his arm.

"No!" the man yells. "Can't you see that you are messing up everything?"

He is very angry.

Turn to page 16.

Good work. You have counted correctly.

As you are carrying a monkey back to the zoo, you hear a cry.

"Help me!" cries a voice. "HELP!"

A tiger is chasing a little boy.

If you try to get to the boy before the tiger does, turn to page 32.

If you go after the tiger, turn to page 24.

You press the superspeed button on your jet pac. As you whiz past the man, you kick the bag out of his hand.

Just then a policeman runs over. "Hey, Dynamo, wait a minute," he yells.

But you do not hear him. You are already far away, looking for new adventures.

Being Dynamo is really great!

The End

You take off your jet pac and strap yourself into a huge chair.

Whoosh! The blast of power forces you back in your chair. Soon, you are traveling at the speed of light.

You look out the window and see the earth. It looks like a beautiful, shiny, blue globe.

Turn to page 13.

You fly closer to town. The buildings and houses are shaking. The bridges are swinging. People are screaming.

Then the shaking stops. The earthquake is over.

You look around. Nothing seems to be damaged.

But wait!

Turn to page 18.

For the first hour of the trip, everything is smooth. But then suddenly the entire space-ship begins to shake.

"Force field!" yells the captain. "We have run into a force field. Don't anybody move."

The ship shakes even worse. You can hear cracking noises.

The ship is breaking apart! you think. *I'd better get my jet pac.*

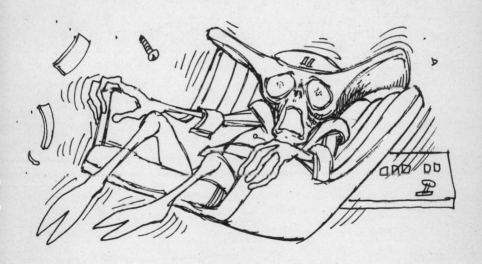

If you get out of the chair and strap on your jet pac, turn to page 20.

If you stay in the chair, turn to page 22.

You fly toward the ship. A huge door slides open and you fly into a room full of strange red creatures. They are bouncing all over the place.

"Are you in trouble?" you ask.

"Glurp," says one alien.

"Flink," says another.

You cannot understand a word they are saying!

One of the aliens comes toward you. She is holding a spiked object in her hand. Sparks are shooting from the points.

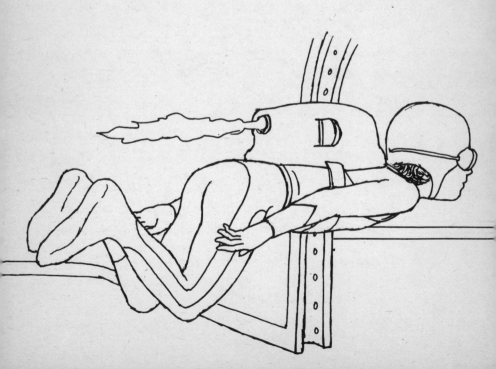

You are very scared.

If you try to grab the weapon, turn to page 26.

If you think that you should stay still, turn to page 27.

"Stop it!" the man screams at you.

"Not until you drop the money," you reply.

There is a crowd of people around you
now.

"Cut!" yells a voice.

"Hey, Dynamo," says another voice. "This
man isn't a robber. He's a movie actor."

You look around. There is a large camera pointing at you.

The people are making a movie. One person begins to laugh. Then another. Soon everyone is laughing. And so are you.

The End

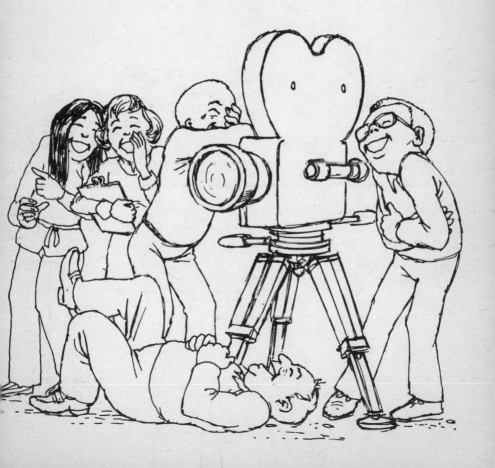

18

As you fly over the zoo, you see that some of the cages have fallen apart. You wonder how many animals are loose.

Look carefully at the picture on these two pages. Hidden in the picture are the escaped animals. Count them. The number of animals is the same as the page number you should turn to next.

(If you can't find the correct number of animals, turn to page 56 for the answer.)

You panic.

You jump from your chair and pick up your jet pac. You begin to strap it on your back.

"Stop!" yells the captain. "Get back in your chair!"

"But if the spaceship breaks apart, I will need my jet pac!" you argue as you finish putting it on.

"Get back in your chair!" the captain yells even louder.

"No!" you scream.

Suddenly the door opens. You feel yourself propelled into space.

Soon you are back on earth. Part of you is glad to be safe. But the other part of you is sad. You will never again have a chance to see an alien planet.

The End

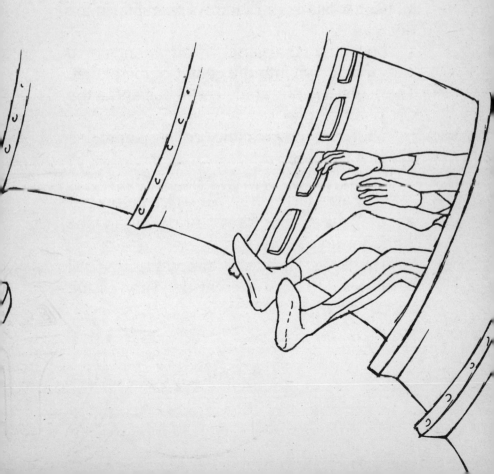

The ship bounces crazily. The cracking noises get worse. But no one does anything. They all just sit there.

Then, all of a sudden, the flight is smooth again.

"Our ship has an automatic force-field device," the captain tells you. "As long as everybody stays still, we are not in trouble."

Soon you see the alien planet in the distance. It looks like a diamond sparkling in the sky.

You land on the planet. Then you ride on a pad of air down into the center of the planet. There you see one shiny metal ball about the size of an orange.

"That ball powers the entire planet," a scientist tells you.

"I wish we had that on earth," you say.

"You are our friend. We will tell you our secrets," the scientist says. "And you can take them home with you."

"Thank you," you say, happy that you will be able to do such a great deed for all the people on earth.

The End

As you fly toward the tiger, it opens its mouth and gets ready to leap at the boy.

I'm too late! you think.

Just then, the boy runs into a building. He is saved!

But you must still take care of the tiger.

You pick up a log and move away from the tiger. Then you fly as fast as you can right at the tiger. Pow! He's out!

When you step back, something squishes under your foot.

If you think it is a rotten banana, turn to page 42.

If you think it is a snake, turn to page 44.

You grab for the weapon. But before you know it, six of the creatures are pointing tiny laser guns at you.
Zap!

Turn to page 28.

You cannot move. The alien puts the object around your neck.

"We will not harm you," she says. "This object is a translator. Now we will understand each other."

"We need your help," says another alien. "We are stuck in the storm."

Suddenly, the spaceship starts to shake violently. Then it begins to fall toward earth. The aliens cannot stop it. They are screaming.

Turn to page 30.

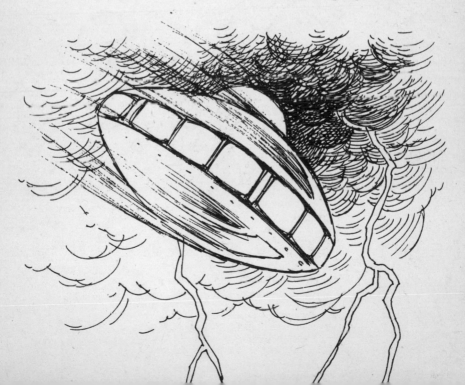

You cannot move. The alien comes toward you. She reaches around your neck with the spiked thing.

You are terrified.

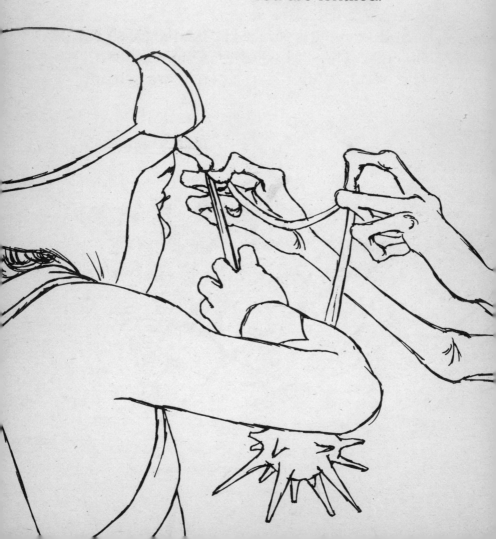

"We will not harm you," says a voice in your head.

Suddenly you realize that the spiked thing is not a weapon. It is a translator.

"We are trapped in the storm," says the voice. You must help us."

Turn to page 35.

You do not know if your jets are powerful enough to save the ship. But you have to try.

You fly through the door. Then you push the emergency-only button on your jet pac.

Power surges out of the jets. You are fighting gravity. And you are winning.

The ship slows down. It lands safely.

When you and the aliens step outside the ship, you are surrounded by human beings.

"Capture the aliens before they harm us!" yells one person.

"Shoot them!" yells another.

"Lock them in jail," screams a third person.

If you try to talk to the crowd, turn to page 40.

If you get the aliens out as fast as you can, turn to page 38.

You do not move. The gorilla sees that you are not going to attack. It stops making terrible noises. It stops beating its chest. It looks at you with gentle, confused eyes.

"Come, gorilla," you say. "I will take you back to the zoo. I won't hurt you, gorilla."

The huge animal follows you back to the zoo. Soon it is playing in its home once more.

The End

You press the green button
and jet to the boy as fast
as you can. The tiger is
right behind him!

You swoop down.
The tiger swipes at
you with its paw.
But it misses.

You scoop up the
boy and fly away.

The boy turns and looks at you.
"Dynamo!" he exclaims. "You
saved my life! You're my hero!"

The End

You fly out into the storm. The spacecraft is shaking badly. You are afraid that it will break apart.

You punch the superspeed button on your jet pac and place both hands on the craft. As power blasts out of your jets, the spaceship begins to move. Higher and higher you go, pushing the ship in front of you.

Faster and faster you fly. Soon, you are out of the storm. You fly back into the ship.

"Thank you," says an alien. "You have saved our lives. In return for this great deed, we invite you to visit our planet."

If you want to go to the alien planet, turn to page 46.

If you do not want to go to an alien planet, you may fly back to the secret door and climb into bed.

The End

You fly to the lava.
You know that the only
way to save the town is to
change the path of the lava.
You look around. Then you have an idea!

Quickly, you unstrap your jet pac. You hold it in your hands. Then you press the high-power, emergency-only button.

The blast from the jet pac begins to dig a hole in the earth.

You fly toward the sea, digging a deep trench as you go. When you get to the ocean, you look back. The lava is flowing harmlessly into the sea.

The town has been saved!

The End

"Quick!" you say. "Get inside and close the door!"

"We cannot leave now," an alien says.

"We must," you say. "We have to get away from these people. I'm afraid they might hurt you."

"How can we fly through such a storm?" asks an alien.

"I will show you," you answer as you all climb into the ship.

The aliens fire the jets. The ship takes off.

You fly right into the storm. The ship shakes violently.

"Fly into the center of the storm," you tell the captain.

"We will be torn apart!" the captain says.

Turn to page 48.

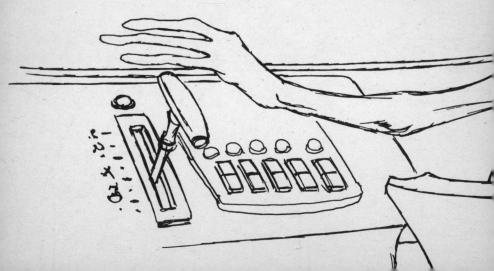

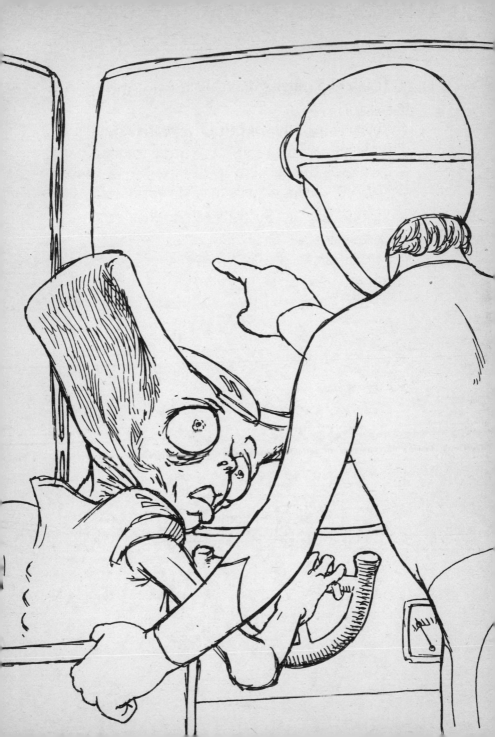

The poor aliens are huddled together in fear.

"Please do not let them harm us," one alien says.

You face the crowd.

"Look!" someone yells. "It's Dynamo!"

"Listen to me!" you yell. "These creatures will not harm you. They are friendly. Let them stay here until the storm passes. Then I will help them take off for home."

"No!" a man yells.

"How do we know we can trust you?" says another.

You look behind you. The aliens are crying.

Turn to page 50.

You guessed wrong. It is a snake! A huge python. And it is wrapping itself around you.

"Oh, no, you don't, Mr. Python," you say to the snake. Then you begin to spin as fast as you can. Your spinning unwinds the snake.

The poor python is so dizzy that you just pick it up and drop it into a tall garbage can. The zoo keeper can come get it later.

You look around for more animals. You don't see any. Then suddenly a huge gorilla runs out of the trees.

Turn to page 52.

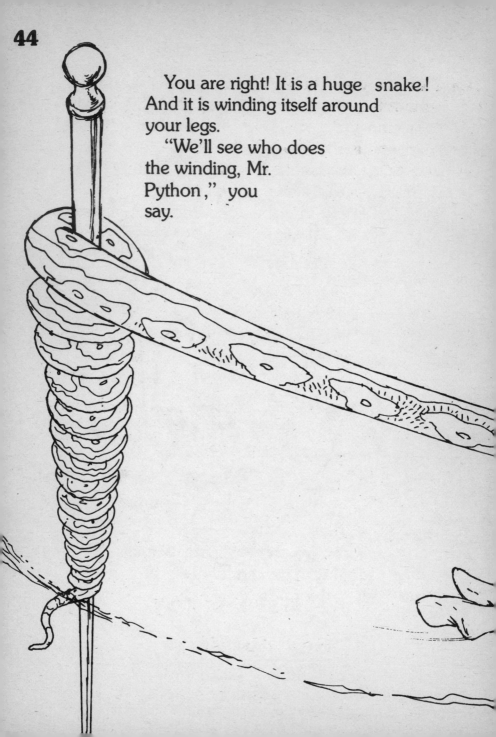

You are right! It is a huge snake!
And it is winding itself around
your legs.

"We'll see who does
the winding, Mr.
Python," you
say.

You grab the python by the head and fly over to a flagpole. You wrap the snake's tail around the pole. Then you fly around and around.

Soon the snake is wrapped around the pole twenty times.

You know that the zoo keeper will figure out how to get the snake back to the zoo.

You are very clever to have found such a fine solution.

The End

You want to go, but you are afraid that you will never see your family again.

"Do not worry," an alien says. "We will bring you home. But there is one very important rule that you must follow if you come with us. You must obey the captain's orders."

You agree to obey the rule.

"Prepare to change course," the captain says. The aliens take their positions.

"Sit down and strap on your seat belt," the captain says to you.

Your heart beats faster.

Turn to page 11.

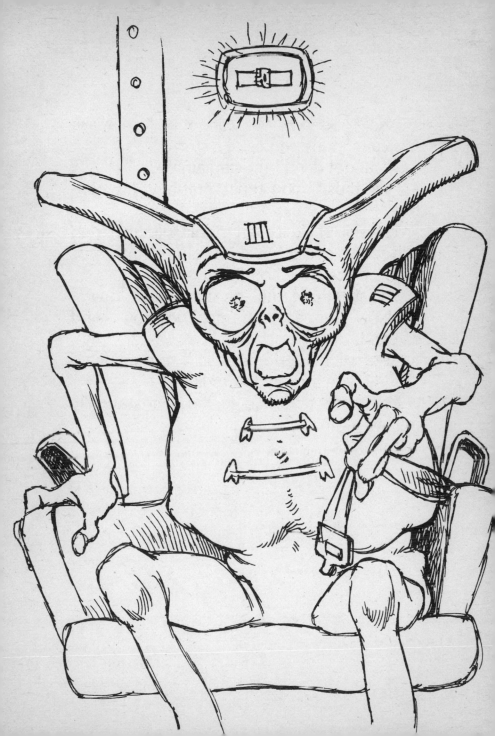

"No," you say. "We will not be torn apart. It is calm in the center of a storm."

"I cannot do it!" the captain yells.

"We must!" you reply, grabbing the controls.

The ship shakes even more violently. Then suddenly everything is calm. You have reached the "eye" of the storm.

You stay there until the storm quiets down.

"Now you can fly home," you say. "And so can I."

"We will never forget you," says an alien. "Thank you for saving our lives."

You wave goodbye to the aliens and fly toward earth.

From out in space, the earth looks blue and peaceful. But as you get closer, you see smoke. And fire.

Then you discover that a volcano is erupting. The hot lava is flowing down a mountain—right toward a town.

If you try to stop the lava from burying the town, turn to page 36.

If you fly to the town to save the people, turn to page 54.

"The aliens will not harm you," you say to the people. "I give you my word of honor."

"Please take us home," says the captain. "We want to go home."

A woman in the crowd says, "This is Dynamo. We can trust Dynamo."

Everyone in the crowd agrees.

You wait with the aliens until the storm passes. Then you tell them that it is safe to fly home.

"We will never forget you," says an alien.

"Me, too," you answer sadly.

You are happy because you have saved their lives, but you are sad that they are going home.

The End

You run toward
the gorilla as fast as you
can. The huge animal sees
you. It stops. Then, with a horrible
roar, the gorilla beats its chest.
It is ready to attack!
    The animal is five
times larger than you are.
Its teeth look deadly.

Turn to page 31.

You fly to the town. People are running all over the place.

In your loudest voice, you tell everybody to gather in the town square. Then one by one you carry each person and fly them to the top of a hill.

By the time the lava reaches the town, everyone is safe.

"Hurray for Dynamo!" yells one person.

"You have saved our lives!" the others yell.

"You are a hero!"

The End

Answer to Puzzle on pages 18 and 19:

1. Kangaroo; 2. Seal; 3. Snake; 4. Monkey; 5. Alligator;
6. Gorilla; 7. Elephant; 8. Tiger; 9. Giraffe

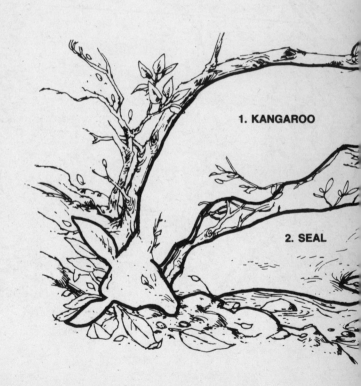

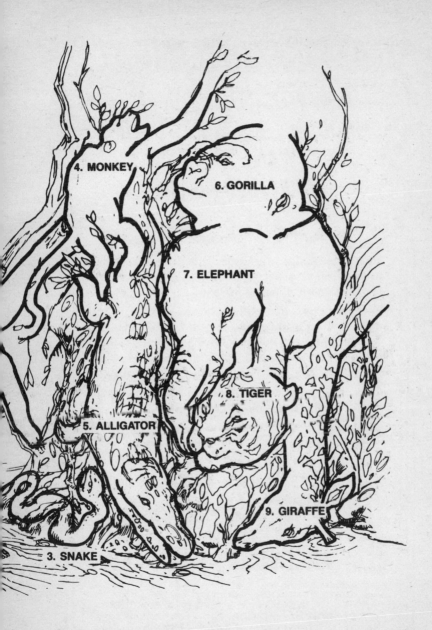